WELL-MANNERED ALEXANDER

WRITTEN BY

SOPHIE ERRANTE

This book belongs to:

_____

PURE
AWESOME
PRESS

A brand of IVA PUBLISHING

Independently published by:
Iva Publishing Bogdan Ivanov
Württembergische Str. 18
10707 Berlin
Germany

You can contact us at hello@ivapublishing.com

ISBN 9798803884439 (Paperback)

Alexander loves cooking a lot.
He loves breaking the eggs and he loves stirring the pot.

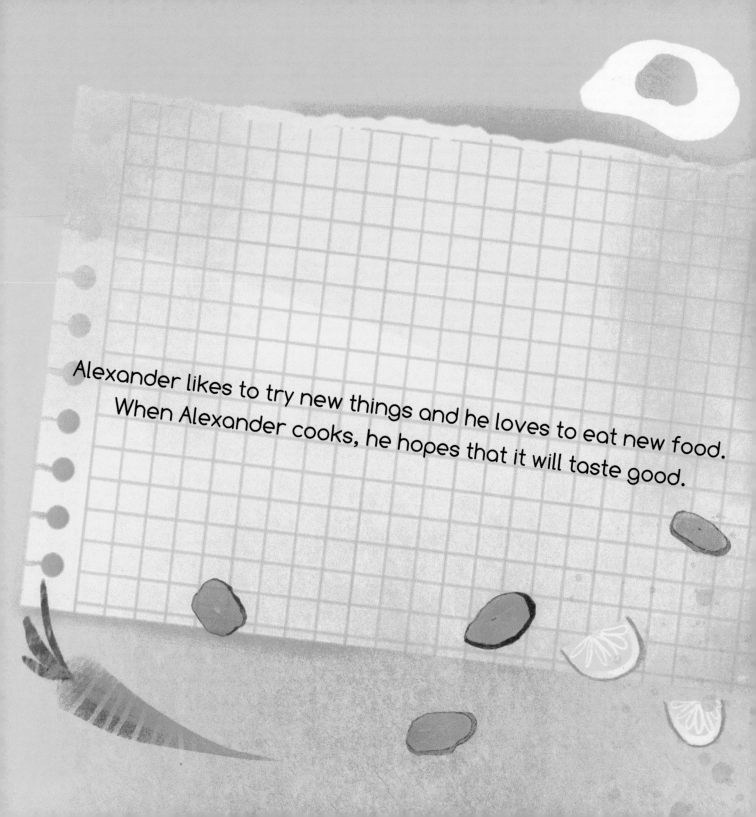

Alexander likes to try new things and he loves to eat new food. When Alexander cooks, he hopes that it will taste good.

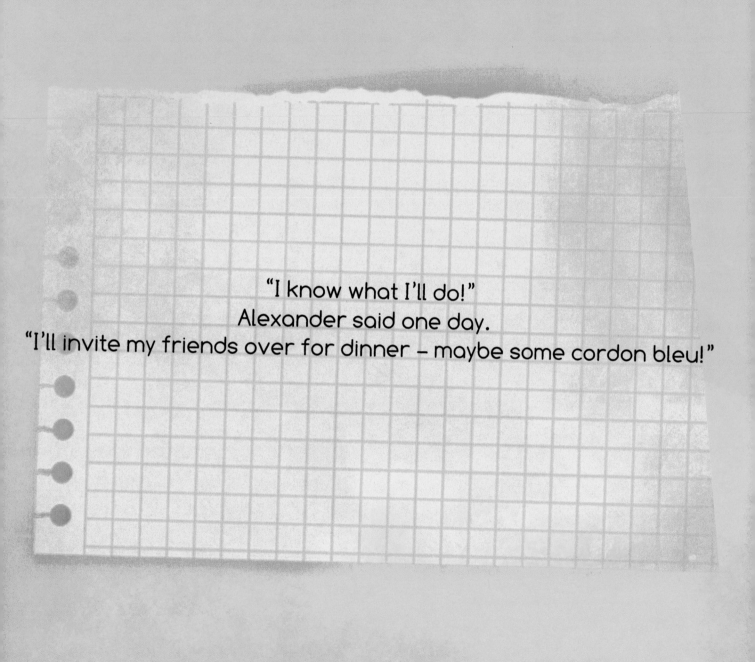

"I know what I'll do!"
Alexander said one day.
"I'll invite my friends over for dinner – maybe some cordon bleu!"

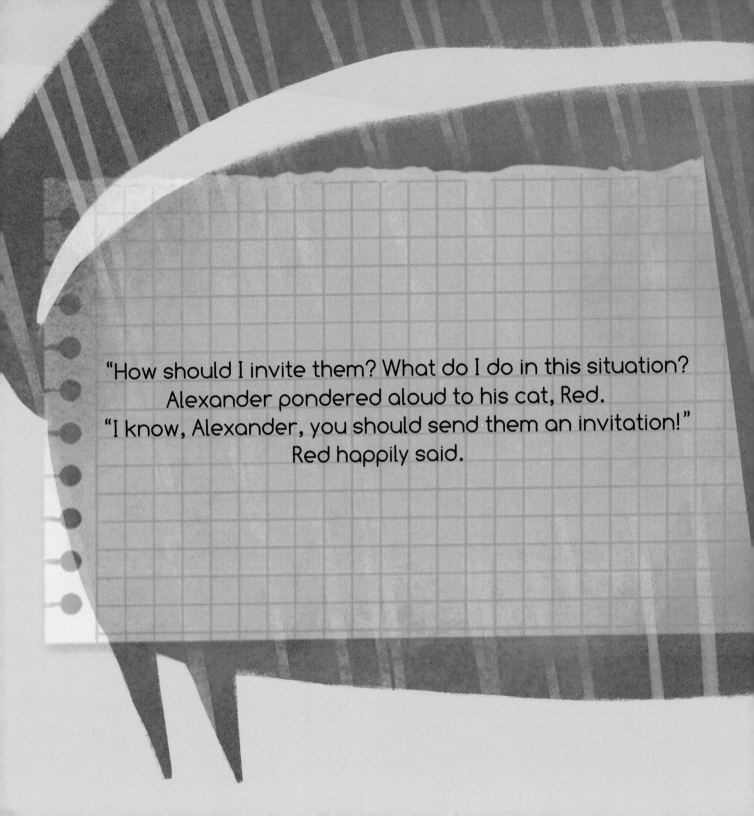

"How should I invite them? What do I do in this situation?
Alexander pondered aloud to his cat, Red.
"I know, Alexander, you should send them an invitation!"
Red happily said.

Alexander began to write,
He wanted to be direct:
"Come over tonight."
But that doesn't seem to connect.

"How do you write an invitation? Do you have to be nice?"

Red replied, "That would be good, be nice and say please."

Alexander wrote: "Please come over tonight. Don't make me ask twice"

"No, don't say that, Alexander! You'll leave them ill at ease!"

"When you say "please" you should be warm like summer weather."
The cat said, "This will help them make the decision together."

"Okay, I've got it!

Come over tonight, please. I'd love to see you."

How does that sound? Did I make a breakthrough?"

"That sounds much better, but there's still room to grow. If I got this invitation I wouldn't know where to go."

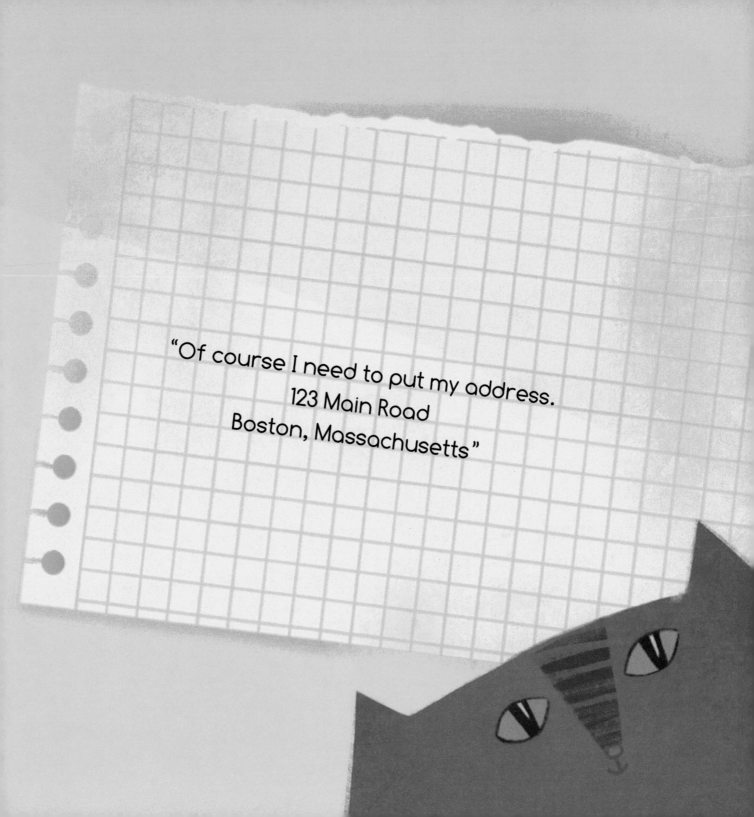

"Of course I need to put my address.
123 Main Road
Boston, Massachusetts"

"You are on your way to being very polite! Let's go through what you will do tonight."

"Invite them in, take their coats and purses,
Help them find a place to sit, and don't say any curses!"

"Smile and offer them something to drink.
Ask them about their lives and their families,
They won't want to yawn or think your parties stink.
All of this will happen if you're sure to say please!"

Manners are important because this is the golden rule:
Treat others like you want to be treated.
Remember to apply this also at school.

And when the party is through,
Call them at home or send them a card,
But one thing stays true:
Always be sure to say "thank you!"

THANK YOU!

for reading Well-Mannered Alexander.
Please consider leaving us a
review on Amazon. Your
opinion is important to us!

Made in the USA
Middletown, DE
10 October 2022

12429972R00020